A Wild Cowboy

Dana Kessimakis Smith ★ Laura Freeman

Jump at the Sun ◉ Hyperion Books for Children / New York

I am a boy, a wild cowboy
A real live buckaroo

I'm fixin' to meet my ranch hand
We've got a job to do

I pack my gear, my cowpoke stuff
I'll need some things for the ride

I'm leavin' town, I'm movin' on
My pardner's by my side

I have a horse, my very own
Her mane is silky black

I mount my horse, I reach and climb
And ride upon her back

We blaze a trail, a twistin' path

We all meet up out West

We move the cattle, we bring them in
We are the frontier's best

We pass the canyon, where bandits hide
"Giddyup! Giddyup!" I say

The others lead the rest of the herd
And I round up the stray

We set up camp, this cowboy's home
A fire flickers and pops

I find some grub, some cowboy food
I eat till the rumblin' stops

It's almost dusk, day turns to night
The coyotes sing with a moan

I look at the sky, twilight up high
The stars blaze a trail of their own

I fetch my bedroll—a blanket or two—
It softened the ground where I lay

A smooch for my horse
and a hug, of course
At the end of a rugged day

I settle on in,
I close my eyes
Morning will
come soon

I am a boy, a wild cowboy
Who sleeps beneath the moon.

Printed in Singapore
First Edition
1 3 5 7 9 10 8 6 4 2
This book is set in 20-point Cantoria.
Reinforced binding
Library of Congress Cataloging-in-Publication Data on file.
ISBN 0-7868-1931-6

Visit www.hyperionchildrensbooks.com

To my mom and dad, the best in the West

*Very special thanks to editor Garen Thomas, whose
belief and vision made this book come to life*
—D.K.S.

*To my three guardian angels:
Anne, Garen, and Jackie . . . your confidence and
understanding strengthen and inspire me*
—L.F.

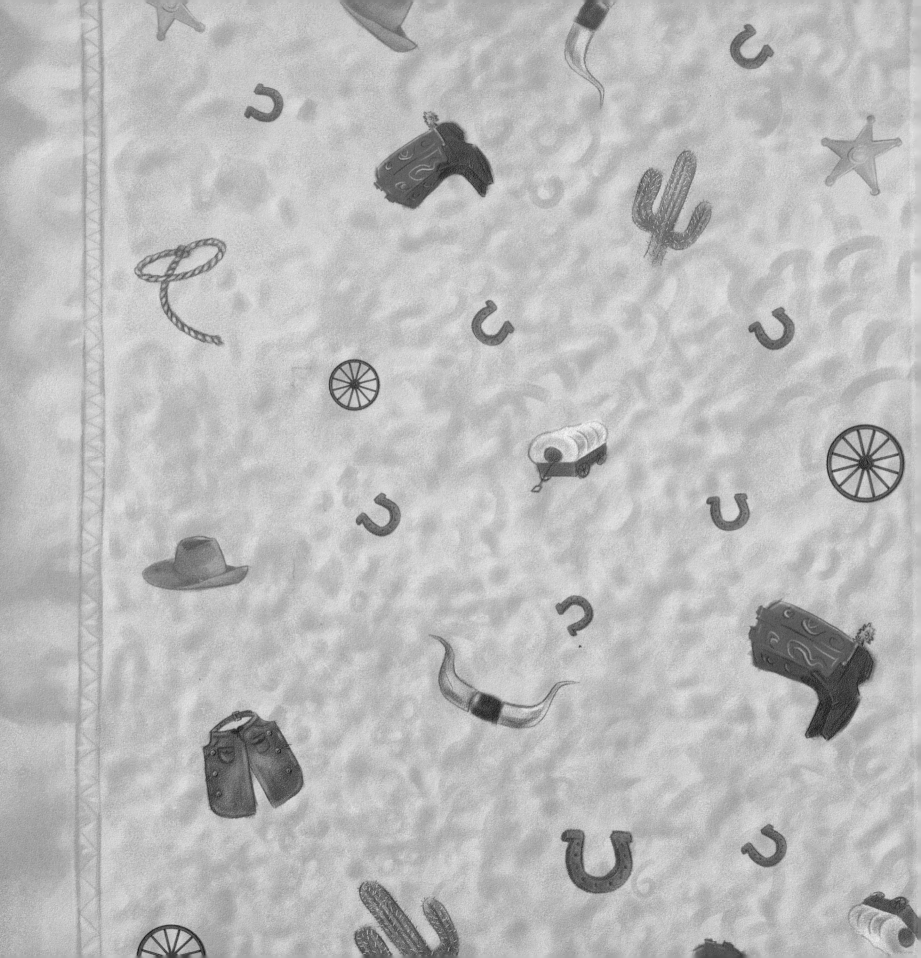